*What would you do if you met a genie? Would you
have your three wishes ready? When I was seven I had
my wishes all picked out. And I made sure that my family
knew about them too, in case they met one. When my
mother wrote out her shopping list – milk, bread, broccoli
– I would add my list for the genie – world peace, a magic
carpet, and long legs for basketball. Well, just in case.*

I've still got my list. And I'm still hoping!

*Tashi was all prepared for a genie, just like me.
But you can never depend on the kind of genie you're
likely to meet. And that was his trouble...*

ANNA FIENBERG

Anna and Barbara Fienberg write the Tashi stories together,
making up all kinds of daredevil adventures and tricky
characters for him to face. Lucky he's such a clever Tashi.

Kim Gamble is one of Australia's favourite illustrators
for children. Together Kim and Anna have made such
wonderful books as *The Magnificent Nose and Other
Marvels*, *The Hottest Boy Who Ever Lived*, the *Tashi* series,
the *Minton* picture books, *Joseph*, and a full colour picture
book about their favourite adventurer, *There once was
a boy called Tashi*.

First published in 1997
This edition first published in 2006

Allen & Unwin
83 Alexander St
Crows Nest NSW 2065
Australia
Phone: (61 2) 8425 0100
Fax: (61 2) 9906 2218
Email: info@allenandunwin.com
Web: www.allenandunwin.com

National Library of Australia
Cataloguing-in-Publication entry:

Fienberg, Anna.
    Tashi and the genie.

    New cover ed.
    For primary school children.
    ISBN 978 1 74114 968 5.

    ISBN 1 74114 968 1.

    1. Children's stories, Australian. 2. Tashi (Fictitious character) – Juvenile
    fiction. I. Fienberg, Barbara. II. Gamble, Kim. III. Title. (Series: Tashi; 4).

A823.3

Cover and series design by Sandra Nobes
Typeset in Sabon by Tou-Can Design
Printed in Australia by McPhersons Printing Group

10 9 8 7 6 5 4 3 2

Tashi
and the
GENIE

written by
Anna
Fienberg

and

Barbara Fienberg

•

illustrated by
Kim Gamble

ALLEN&UNWIN

Jack and Tashi ran up the wharf and
hurtled onto the ferry. They flung themselves
down on a seat outside, just as the boat
chugged off.

Tashi watched the white water foam behind
them. The sun was warm and gentle on
their faces. Jack closed his eyes.

'What a magical day!' they heard a woman say as she brushed past them. Jack's eyes snapped open.

'Talking of magic,' he said to Tashi, 'let's hear about the time you saw that genie. What did he look like? How did you meet him?'

'Well,' said Tashi, taking a breath of sea air,
'it was like this. One day, not long before I
came to this country, I was in the shed
looking for some nails. Grandmother called
me, saying she wanted a few eggs. I
gathered about four or five from under the
hens and then looked around for a dish to
put them in. I spied an old, cracked one on
a top shelf, covered with a dirty piece of
carpet. But there was something very
strange about this bowl.'

'Ooh,' squealed Jack.

'I know, I know
what was in it!'

'Yes,' nodded Tashi. 'When I lifted the
carpet I saw a bubbling grey mist inside;
soft rumbling snores were coming from it.
The snores turned to a splutter when I
poked it. A voice groaned, "Oh not again!
Not already!" And the mist swirled and
rose up in the air. Two big sleepy eyes
squinted down at me. "And only twenty-five
years and ten minutes since my last master
let me go!" it said. Well, I was *very* excited.'

'Who *wouldn't* be,' Jack agreed.

'"You're a genie!" I shouted.

'"What if I am?" said he.

'"Why aren't you in a bottle?" I asked. "Or a lamp, like normal genies?"

'The genie looked shifty. "Oh, my master went off in too much of a hurry to put me back in my lamp. So I just crept into this bowl, hoping for some peace and quiet."'

Tashi winked at Jack. 'I happened to know a lot about genies, because my grandmother was always telling me what to do if I met one. So I looked him in the eye and said, "Now that I've found you, don't you have to grant me three wishes?"'

'The genie groaned. "Wishes, wishes! People don't realise they are usually better off leaving things the way they are." But he pulled himself up to his full height and straightened his turban. "What is your command, master?" he bowed.

'I thought for a moment. "I would like an enormous sack of gold." Imagine, I could build a splendid palace, for all my family to live in.

'The genie snapped his fingers and—
TA RA—a sack of gold lay at my feet! I ran my hands through the glittering coins and held one up. Hmm, before I build the palace, I thought, I might just run down to the sweet-maker's shop.'

'Good idea!' cried Jack. 'You could buy a *million* sweets, to last you till you're a hundred and ten!'

'Yes, but when Second Cousin at the shop took my coin, she looked at it carefully and rubbed it on her sleeve. The gold rubbed right off. "This coin is no good, Tashi," she told me. "It's only copper."

'I stamped back to the shed and angrily shook the genie out of his dish. "Those coins are only copper!" I shouted.

'The genie yawned. "Really? All of them? How tragic." He stretched. "Maybe a few at the bottom will be gold. What I need now is a glass of tea before I do any more work."'

'What a lousy, lazy genie!' exploded Jack.

'Yes,' agreed Tashi. 'And it gets worse. By the time I'd brought his tea, I'd thought of my second wish. "What about a flying carpet?" I asked. Oh, if only I'd known. The genie looked at me doubtfully. "Flying carpets are not my best thing," he said. But I was firm with him, so he snapped his fingers, and there, floating at my knees, was a glittering carpet. It was the most magnificent thing I had ever seen. All smooth and polished as skin, it was patterned with hundreds of tiny peacocks, with eyes glowing like jewels.

'The carpet trembled as I climbed on. The genie showed me how to tug at the corners to steer it. And then we were off, the carpet and I, out of the shed, over the house and across the village square. All the people were amazed, as they looked up and saw me waving at them.'

'I bet they were!' cried Jack. 'My dad would have fainted with shock. So, did you get to see Africa? Or Spain?'

'No,' Tashi frowned. 'It was like this. I had just turned in the direction of Africa, in fact, when the carpet suddenly dipped and bucked like a wild horse. My knees slipped right to the edge! I threw myself face down on the carpet, grabbing hold of the fringe.

'The carpet heaved up and down, and side to side, trying to throw me off. A hundred times it kicked me in the belly, but I clung on. The world was swirling around me like soup in a pot, and then I saw we were heading straight for the willow tree beside my house. I came crashing down through the branches. When I got my breath back, I marched off to find the genie.

'"Well, you certainly aren't very good at your job, are you?" I scolded as I brushed the leaves from my hair.'

'Is that all you could say?' yelled Jack. 'I would have called him a fumble-bumble *beetle*-brain at the very least.'

'Yes, but I still wanted my third wish,' Tashi sighed. 'Oh, if only I'd known. Well, the genie just yawned at me and said, "What is your third—and last—wish, master?"

'I thought carefully. One thing I had often longed for was to meet Uncle Tiki Pu, my father's Younger Brother. He had run away to the city while he was still a boy, but my father had told me stories of his pranks and jokes. "Yes, that's it!" I said. "I would like to meet my Uncle Tiki Pu."

'It was suddenly very quiet in the shed. The genie rose up and clicked his fingers. Nothing happened. "You will find him in your bedroom," said the genie, and slithered back into his bowl. I ran to my bedroom and there was my uncle, stretched out on my bed.

'"Ah, Tashi," he said, "it's about time someone came to find me. My life has been very hard in the city." Before I could say that I was sorry to hear it, and how pleased the family would be to have him back home again, Uncle Tiki Pu went on. "This bed is very hard, however."

'I looked around the room. "Where will *I* sleep, Uncle?"

'"Who knows?" he answered in a bored voice. "Get me something to eat, Tashi, a little roast duck and ginger will do. And tell your mother when she comes home that these clothes need washing."

'He pointed to a pile of his clothes beside my toy box. The lid was open and inside my box were jars of hair oil and tins of tobacco instead of my train set and kite and rock collection.

'"Where are my things?" I cried.

'"Oh, I threw them out the window," he told me. "How else could I make room for my belongings?"

'I ran outside and gathered up my toys. Two wheels had fallen off my little red train. "What about *my* belongings?" I called through the window.

'"Don't worry about them," replied Uncle
Tiki Pu. "You won't be living here much
longer. This house is too small for all of us
now that I've come back. You can have my
old job in the city, Tashi. But mind you take
a rug to sleep on because they don't give
you any bedding there, and the stony
ground is crawling with giant spiders that
bite. See, I've got the wounds to prove it."

'And he lifted his holey old singlet to show big red lumps all over his tummy, like cherry tomatoes.

'"Do they give you food in the city?" I could hardly bear to ask.

'"No, there's never enough, so you have to hunt for it. That's where the spiders come in handy. If you squish them first, they're not bad in a fritter. Oh, and watch out for alligators—they swim in the drains. Well, goodbye and good luck! You'll need it, ha ha!" And he laughed a wicked laugh.'

Tashi stopped for a moment, because he couldn't help shivering at the terrible memory of his uncle, and also because Jack was jumping up and down on his seat in outrage. The woman who had said 'What a magical day!' was staring.

'I know,' said Tashi. 'I know, I couldn't believe it either, that a member of my family could be so evil. My head was pounding, and I ran straight to see the genie.'

'How could *he* help, that old *beetle*-brain?'

'Well,' said Tashi. 'It was like this. I picked up his bowl and tried to wake the genie again. I shook him and begged him to get rid of Uncle Tiki Pu, but he just closed his eyes tightly and said, "Go away, Tashi. You've had your three wishes and that's that." Suddenly I put the bowl down and smiled. I had just had a cunning idea. I remembered another thing Grandmother always told me about genies.

'I hurried back to my room and said to Uncle Tiki Pu, "You are quite right. This house is very small and poky. How would you like to live in a palace instead?"

'Uncle Tiki Pu sat up with a bounce. "Just what I've always wanted!" he cried. "How did you *know*?"

'"Come with me," I told him, "and I will show you how to do it."

'I opened the door of the shed and led him to the genie's bowl. Uncle let out a howl of joy when he saw what was curled up inside, but when the genie rose into the air, his eyes weren't sleepy any more. They were bright and sly.

'"I am your new master, so listen carefully, Genie," Uncle Tiki Pu began. "For my first wish—"

'The genie interrupted him. "There will be no wishes for you, my friend. You really should have been more careful. Don't you know that every seventh time a genie is disturbed, *he* becomes the master, and the one who wakes him must be the slave?" He glided over and arranged himself on Uncle Tiki Pu's shoulders. "Take me to the city," he commanded, "and be quick about it."

'Uncle Tiki Pu's face was bulging with rage
and his knees sagged, but he staggered out
of the shed with his load. As he sailed past,
the genie turned and gave me a big wink.
'"Look out for alligators!" I called.'

Jack was quiet for a moment, thinking. He watched people stand up and stretch as the ferry slowed, nearing the city.

'I hope nothing with teeth lives in *our* drains,' he said. 'Well, Tashi, that's amazing! Did you really fly on a magic carpet?'

For an answer, Tashi opened the top buttons
of his jacket, showing Jack the gold coin
hanging on a cord around his neck. 'How
else would I have this?' he said.

And the two boys stepped off the ferry and
strolled over to the ice-cream stand at the
end of the wharf.

Jack burst into the kitchen. 'Tashi's back!' he cried.

'Oh, good,' said Dad. 'Has he been away?'

'Yes, I *told* you,' said Jack, 'don't you remember? He went back to the old country to see his grandmother for the New Year holiday. And while he was there, something terrible happened.'

'His grandmother ran away with the circus?' suggested Dad.

'No,' said Jack. 'She can't juggle. But listen, you know the war lord who came looking for Tashi last year?'

'Yes, I do remember him,' said Dad. 'He was the only war lord in Wilson Street last summer, so I won't forget him in a hurry.'

'Yes, and guess what,' Jack began, but Mum interrupted him.

'Come and have some afternoon tea, while you tell us,' she said, and brought a tray into the living room.

'Well,' said Jack, when they were settled comfortably. 'It was like this. When Tashi arrived back in his village, it was all quiet. *Strangely* quiet. None of his old friends

were playing in the square, and he could
hear someone crying. His grandfather told
him that the war lord had just made a raid
through the village. He'd captured nearly all
the young men for his army—and he had
kidnapped six children as well!'

'What did he take the *children* for?'
asked Mum.

'So that the men would fight bravely and
not run away home,' Jack told her. 'If they
didn't fight, he was going to punish
the children.'

'He deserves to be fried in a fritter, that war
lord!' exploded Dad.

'Yes,' agreed Jack. 'Well, just then the Wan twins came running back into the village square,

'They had hidden while the soldiers seized the young men. Then they'd followed the war party to see where their uncles were being taken.

'The twins said that the children had been put in the dungeon of the war lord's palace. The twins searched and climbed and tapped and dug, but they could find no way in. They said the children were lost forever.

'Everybody in the square listened to the
Wan twins' story, and a dreadful moaning
began. The sound of sadness rose and
swelled like a wave. Parents and aunties and
cousins hung onto each other as if they were
drowning. Then, one by one, people turned
to Tashi. He had once worked for the war
lord in that very palace.'

'Uh oh,' Dad shook his head. 'I bet he was wishing that he had gone on holidays another time.'

'Not Tashi,' said Jack. 'He slipped away to think, and when he returned he went to his grandfather's box of firecrackers and filled his pockets. Then he set off for the palace of the war lord.

By evening, he reached the field where the soldiers were camped.

'He crept past the guards and found the uncles. They were miserable, sitting silent and cold, far from the cooking fires. Tashi whispered to them that they must get ready to leave at any moment, as he was on his way to the dungeon. One man clung to him, crying, "My little sister is only five years old, Tashi. She will be so frightened. You must find the children." Tashi promised to be back by morning.

'Then he went on alone. He remembered a secret passage into the palace that he'd discovered when he was living there before. You entered in a cave nearby and came out through a wardrobe in the war lord's very own bedroom.'

'Ugh,' shuddered Mum. 'I'd rather be anywhere in the world than *there*.'
'I know,' shivered Dad. 'A man like that, you can imagine how his socks smell.'

'Well, anyway,' Jack went on, 'Tashi found
the cave and pulled aside the bushes
covering the entrance. He ran through the
damp tunnel and held his breath as he
pushed at the wardrobe door. It creaked.
What if the war lord had just come upstairs
to get a sharper sword?'

'Or change his socks?' put in Dad.

'Tashi held his breath. He peeped around
the door. The room was empty. He tiptoed
out into the hall and down the stairs. At the
last step he stopped. He felt the firecrackers
in his pockets, and quivered. A daring plan
had popped into his head. But, he
wondered, was he brave enough to do it?

'Instead of going further down the stairs into the dungeon, he found his way along to the kitchens. The cooks were busy preparing a grand dinner for the war lord and didn't notice Tashi as he crawled behind the oil jars and around the rice bins.'

'What was he doing?' asked Mum.
'Having a little snack, of course,' said Dad, taking a bite of Jack's scone.

'You'll find out if you pay attention,' said Jack, and he moved his scone to the other hand. 'When Tashi left the kitchen he could hear the cries of the children, and the sound of their sobbing led him down to the dungeon. Two guards were talking outside the dark, barred room where the children were held. Tashi hopped into an empty barrel close by and called out in a great loud voice, *"The war lord is a beetle-brain!"*'

'*NO!*' cried Mum and Dad together.

'*YES!*' crowed Jack. 'The guards jumped as if they'd just sat on a nest of soldier ants. "One of those pesky children has managed to get out!" the fat guard hissed. "Then we'd better catch him," said the other, "before the war lord boils us in spider sauce."

'As soon as they ran off, Tashi turned the big key they had left in the lock and opened the dungeon door.

'The children recognised Tashi and crowded around, telling him all that had happened. "Shush," whispered Tashi, "wait till we get outside. The danger isn't over yet."

'He led them quickly up the stairs and through the long hallways until at last they came to the great wooden front door of the palace. Tashi reached up and pulled on the big brass latch. The door swung open and the children whooped with joy. They streamed out, falling over each other in their hurry. Tashi picked up the littlest one and set him on his feet. "Home we go!" he cried.

'But no. Just then a huge hand reached down and plucked Tashi up by the collar. He was face to face with the furious war lord. Their noses almost touched. The war lord's skin was rough, like sandpaper.

"*RUN!*" Tashi called to the children. "Run to your uncles down by the camp!"

'The war lord shook Tashi, as if he were a scrap of dirty washing. His iron knuckles bit into Tashi's neck. He breathed fish and grease into Tashi's face. "So, you foolish boy," he growled. "You have come back. You won't escape again. Look well at the daylight outside, for this is the last time you'll see it. You'll work in the dungeons from now on."

'Tashi thought of the mean black bars on the window of the dungeon. Only a cockroach could stay alive in there. His eyes began to water and he started to sniff.

'"Scared, are you?" the war lord jeered.
'"No, I can smell something,"
said Tashi, "can't you?"'
'Socks!' cried Dad.

'The war lord sniffed. The air *did* seem rather smoky. Suddenly there was a loud explosion and they heard feet pounding over the stone floor. "Fire!" shouted the war lord, and he dropped Tashi and ran off towards the noise, calling for the guards to follow him.

'Tashi sped down the steps and soon found the children and their uncles. They were waiting for him over the hill, beyond the camp. From there they had a good view of the palace.

'It was blazing fiercely—the windows were red with the glow of fire inside, and a great grey cloud of smoke climbed above it.

'"Weren't we lucky the fire started just then!" said the littlest boy. His brother laughed and looked at Tashi. "I don't think luck had anything to do with it," he said.

'"Well," said Tashi modestly, "as a matter of fact I did empty the gunpowder out of my firecrackers and laid a trail up to the kitchen stove. I hoped we would manage to get out before it reached the ovens. It blew up just in time."

'"What a clever Tashi!" the children yelled, and the uncles hoisted him up onto their shoulders and they sang and danced all the way home.

'Phew!' said Dad. 'That was a close shave. I suppose Tashi could relax after that, and enjoy the rest of his holiday. Did he have good weather?'

'Yes, at first,' said Jack, 'until the witch,
Baba Yaga, blew in on the winds of a
dreadful storm.'

'Baba Yaga?' said Dad nervously. 'Who is she?'

'Oh, just a witch whose favourite meal is
baked children. But Tashi will tell us all about
that. What's for dinner tonight, Mum?'